THOMAS & FRIENDS™

RUNAWAY ENGINE!

Illustrated by Tommy Stubbs

Random House 🏠 New York

Thomas the Tank Engine & Friends™

CREATED BY BRITT ALLCROFT

Based on The Railway Series by The Reverend W Awdry.
© 2011 Gullane (Thomas) LLC.

Thomas the Tank Engine & Friends and Thomas & Friends are trademarks of Gullane (Thomas) Limited.
HIT and the HIT Entertainment logo are trademarks of HIT Entertainment Limited.

3-D special effects by Red Bird Press. All rights reserved.

ISBN: 978-0-375-87253-2

www.randomhouse.com/kids   www.thomasandfriends.com

MANUFACTURED IN CHINA   10 9 8 7 6 5 4 3 2 1

HiT entertainment

One day, high in the hills of the Island of Sodor, Thomas the Tank Engine made an amazing discovery.

Thomas found an old town. It was overgrown with ivy and the buildings were crumbling.

"I cannot wait to tell everyone about this!" he peeped.

"Thomas, you have made a wonderful discovery," Sir Topham Hatt said. "This was the town of Great Waterton."

"It once had wonderful springs," Sir Topham Hatt told Thomas. "But when the water dried up, the people moved away. We must repair the town in time for Sodor Day!"

Because Thomas had discovered the town, Sir Topham Hatt put him in charge of the repairs. Thomas wanted to show everyone that he was Really Useful, so he worked very hard. Maybe *too* hard. . . .

One morning, Thomas had an accident! He was puffing too
fast along an old track and toppled off the rickety rails. It took
hours to hoist him back onto the tracks.

Thomas went to the Sodor Steamworks to be fixed. While he was there, Stanley was put in charge of the Great Waterton repairs. Thomas wasn't worried.

"When I'm all fixed, I'm sure I'll get my job back," he tooted.

But when Thomas returned to Great Waterton, Sir Topham Hatt said Stanley would stay in charge of the work.
Thomas' funnel flattened.

"It's not fair," Thomas thought. "I found the town—
I should be in charge."

Thomas had an idea. He'd find something new, and then
everyone would see he was more Useful than Stanley. He
remembered seeing an old mine nearby.

The mine was dark. The rails were old and twisty. Thomas whizzed through the tunnels. Suddenly, he lost control on a steep hill and flew off the tracks!

Thomas was lost deep underground. Would anyone hear his whistle?

Back in Great Waterton, Stanley needed Thomas to shunt some freight cars—but Thomas was nowhere to be found. Stanley went looking for him. At the end of some old tracks, he heard a whistle peeping inside an abandoned mine.

"Stanley, I'm so glad you found me!" tooted Thomas.
Stanley pulled the little blue engine onto the rails.
But there was a loud *POP* and a hiss of steam.

Stanley's hard work had made him burst a valve.

"It's my turn to help you!" Puff by puff, Thomas pushed his new friend out of the mine.

Thomas knew that if they worked together, the repairs at Great Waterton would be done in no time.

Sodor Day finally arrived. There was a big party to reopen Great Waterton.

"Thomas, you've done an excellent job," said Sir Topham Hatt.

"I couldn't have done it without Stanley," puffed Thomas. The two engines peeped happily, and everyone cheered.

WELCOME TO GREAT WATERTON

STANLEY

1